LINDA H

# The Adventures of
# Phantom and Shadow

## Frog Song

To order additional copies of this book, contact:
Xlibris
1-888-795-4274
www.Xlibris.com
Orders@Xlibris.com

ISBN:   Softcover        978-1-7960-6568-8
        EBook            978-1-7960-6567-1

Print information available on the last page

Rev. date: 10/11/2019

# The Adventures of
# Phantom and Shadow

## Frog Song

To
Benjamin and Jason Reece
Spencer and Jolie Hall
Liam and James Dowton
Keep on listening

"Hey Phantom, come look at what I found," hollered Shadow.

"Now what are you doing?" I'm busy trying to take a nap."

"In the sun?" asked Shadow

"Yes, in the sun. What do you want?" replied Phantom.

"You sure are a lazy dog. Just come see what I found in the grass here under the tree."

"Oh, all right."

As Phantom got up and approached Shadow, under the tree, he saw something green and shiny in the grass.

"What is that?" asked Phantom.

"I'm not sure," answered Shadow who moved closer and gave the shiny thing a sniff and a big sloppy lick.

"Excuse me, do you mind not slobbering on me?" asked the green, shiny thing.

Phantom jumped back and shouted, "Who are you and what are you?"

"No need to shout. My name is Bosco and I am a frog. Who, may I ask, are you?"

"My name is Phantom, and this is my friend Shadow."

"What are you two creatures? You certainly are not frogs," replied Bosco rudely.

"Well no, we are dogs, and this is our home. Where are you from?"

"Well, I have heard of your kind but have never met any of you. You are rather strange looking."

"You should talk," said Phantom, "You are strange looking yourself."

Shadow gave Bosco another sloppy lick.

"Do you mind not doing that? My home is in the pond, over the fence and
across the railroad tracks. I desperately want to go home."

"What is keeping you from leaving?" asked Phantom, as he turned with head and tail held high.

"I can't get across the fence or railroad tracks by myself, I am too small."

"Then how did you get all the way over here?" asked Shadow

"A little boy found me in the pond and brought me here. He put me in a glass bowl with water and a rock, not a very good home for a frog. After a day, he became bored with me and went to find something else to play with. I wish he had left me in the pond with my family." replied Bosco, sounding sad.

"How did you get out of the bowl?" asked Shadow.

"I hopped on the rock and jumped out. I made my way over here to rest in the shade while I tried to decide what to do next. Then the that big slobber dog found me."

"Do you know your way home for sure?" asked Phantom.

"I already told you I do. Boy, you sure aren't too smart," replied Bosco.

"Well, we were going to try and help you get home but with an attitude like that you can forget it," said Shadow

Then Phantom and Shadow went into their house for a drink of water, something to eat, and to take a nap.

That night Shadow was awakened by the saddest sound he had ever heard. He woke up Phantom and told him to listen.

"It sounds like a sad song. Where is it coming from?"

"Somewhere outside, let's go see if we can find what is making the sound." Replied Shadow

"Do we have to?" asked Phantom, who didn't like to go out in the dark.

"You'll be ok, you'll be with me."

Shadow went through their doggie door first and stood silently on the deck.

"It is coming from over there, by the tree."

Phantom went through the door to join Shadow. As they got closer to the tree, they realized it was Bosco who was singing so sadly.

"Your song is the saddest I have ever heard," said Phantom.

"I can't help it. I can hear my family over in the pond and I can't get to them. I am sad by myself. I miss my family. Won't you please help me get home?"

Phantom and Shadow looked at each other and decided that they would help Bosco return to his family in the pond.

"How can we help?" they asked.

"Get me over the fence and the railroad tracks to the forest with the pond. Please."

"How will we get him over all this?" Shadow asked Phantom.

"You could carry him on your head," said Phantom.

"Why me, why not you?" asked Shadow in wonderment.

"Don't be silly, your head is much bigger than mine."

Shadow lay down in the grass and Bosco climbed onto his head, with a little nose push from Phantom.

"Wow, I have never been up this high before. I sure can see a lot," said Bosco excitedly.

Then the three of them were off to get Bosco back to his family.

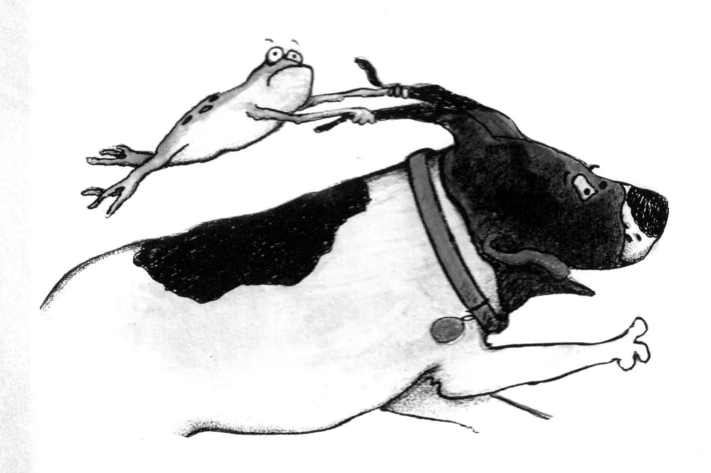

They made it across the yard and to the fence but when Shadow jumped the fence Bosco fell off his head.

"Hey, come back, I am down here."

Shadow and Phantom went back for him.

"Well, that didn't work, now what?" asked Shadow.

"You could carry him in your mouth." Replied Phantom.

"I am willing to try anything."

So, Shadow lay down in the grass and Bosco climbed into his mouth.

"Whew, it stinks in here," said Bosco,

"You don haste o ood either," mumbled Shadow

After they got over the fence Phantom asked, "Which way now?"

"Go over the railroad tracks in front of us and make sure to look both ways for a train."

After reaching the tracks, they looked both ways and did not see a train, so they continued on their journey. They were heading towards the sound of the frogs singing, but before they reached the pond the singing stopped.

"Oh no, now what do we do? If they stay quiet, we may not find them," cried Bosco. "I know the home is around here, but I have never come back without my family being along."

"Call to them and ask them to keep singing. Let them know you are here and trying to find them," suggested Phantom.

"Family, it is me! Keep singing so I can find you," shouted Bosco.

Suddenly the frogs sang even louder. It took no time at all to for the three of them to find the pond and Bosco's family.

As the three of them emerged from the trees to a clearing they saw the pond. Their first sight was of Bosco's mom and brother sitting on a log rejoicing.

"Oh my son, I didn't think I would ever see you again. I am so happy you are home."

"I missed you!" said Bosco.

"What are these creatures that brought you home?" asked his mother.

"They are my new friends. Phantom is the little one and Shadow is the big one with bad breath. They are dogs."

"I will be forever grateful to you for getting my son home safely."

"It was our pleasure," replied Phantom. Shadow was busy getting a drink of water to rinse out the taste of frog.

Phantom and Shadow stayed and played with Bosco and his family in the pond. The frogs took turns getting rides on Shadows head, but not in his mouth. Shadow promised himself he would never give another mouth ride, ever.

After a while the dogs decided to head home so their humans would not miss them and get worried. Before they left Bosco thanked them, and they promised to visit as often as they could.

On the way home, they heard the frogs singing, and Phantom said to Shadow, "It is strange, when only Bosco was singing it sounded so sad, but when a whole family of frog sing it is a beautiful song."

"Indeed," replied Shadow.

From then on Phantom and Shadow sat every night on the deck and listened to the beautiful singing of the frogs. They called it "Frog Song".

Stay tuned for more adventures
coming your way!!

CPSIA information can be obtained
at www.ICGtesting.com
Printed in the USA
BVHW021441231019
580BV00007B/50/P